MAL

JILL PATON WALSH

Thomas *and* *the* Tinners

Illustrated by ALAN MARKS

WAYLAND

Chapter One

Some while ago there was a ferryman, who earned his living rowing people to and fro across the mouth of a river, where it joined the sea. And the ferryman had a daughter who was little and light, and sang as she looked for mussels along the shore, or pinned up the linen to dry, so her father and mother called her Birdy.

Every morning of the year, except for Sundays, the bal-men and bal-maidens, who worked in the tin mine, came down to the bank of the river, and hailed Birdy's father, and he rowed the boat across to fetch them. Then they climbed the hill opposite and went to work in the mine, fetching up and finishing tin to make into shining ingots.

There was Steady Jack who held the
borer, and Hefty Jack who hit the borer
with a hammer till it made a deep hole in
the rock, and Careful Jack who packed the
gunpowder in the hole, and Fire Jack who
lit the fuse, and Standback Jack who cried
the warning, and when each had done his
part there was a flash of light, and a big
bang, and the black tin came tumbling
down from the walls of the tunnel, and
everyone shovelled and carted it away and
pulled it up with ropes and pulleys till it
came to grass.

And every man jack of the miners had a candle stuck in a clay ball on his hatcap, and a pair of spare candles hanging from his buttonhole by the uncut wicks.

They all needed something to eat at croust time, and so every morning Birdy's mother baked nice big pasties, and Birdy helped her fold them and crimp them into shape. Every morning the tinners bought them on the way by.

And then one morning when the tinners came by there was a new boy with them – a scrap of a boy, not much bigger than Birdy. Careful Jack said, "This is Prentice Jack, come to be the fetch and carry man, and help us at our tasks, and can he have a pasty too this morning?"

Prentice Jack said, "My name is Thomas, really. And I can't have a pasty that I haven't a penny to pay for."

"You'll only need a little one," said Birdy. "Have mine, and I'll bake me another, and paying will keep till your wage-day."

Thomas thanked her, and off he went, last in line up the grassy hill to the mine.

Chapter Two

It was dark and dirty down in the mine, in the maze of tunnels, and the holes in the floors that dropped to darker passages further down, and there was lots of climbing on tippy trembling ladders up and down, and that with baskets of heavy ore on your back. The hammering and blasting made your ears ring, and the dust ringed round the bal-mens' lips and eyes and nostrils, and made them look strangely.

Thomas didn't know what he should call things. He didn't know that a bucket of tin was called a kibbleful, and the shafts were called winzes, and the time they spent down the mine was a core, and his lunch break was croust time. People kept shouting at him and telling him things. Thomas hated it.

Just once he asked a question of his own. When all the nearby banging and hammering stopped for a moment, there was a tiny faint ringing and pattering noise, as though he could hear another team of workers faintly through the thick of the rock, or as though a battering of raindrops was ringing on a tin roof a little distance off.

"What's that?" asked Thomas, and Jack
the tribute man told him it was the fairy
miners – the Buccas – who must be working
a tiny seam somewhere nearby.

"What do they look like?" asked
Thomas.

"We don't see them; and it's only one day
in twenty we hear them, either," said Jack.
He was smiling and Thomas thought
perhaps it was a leg-pull.

"Back to work now," said Jack. It
seemed to go on for ever, and Thomas
couldn't believe when croust time came
that it was only half-way through the day.

The men all sat on benches in one of the
tunnels right where they were working, and
Jack the tribute man passed the water
barrel round from hand to hand, and each
man unwrapped his pasty, and began to
eat.

Thomas sat on the very end of the croust bench, next to the darkness, and furthest from the candles. He was so miserable that there was a channel washed clean by tears on both his dirty cheeks. He got out his own little pasty, and did it smell good!

And he had no sooner unwrapped the golden crust, and opened his mouth for the first bit, than he heard a faint little voice from somewhere beside his shoes, saying *"Not so fast! Not so hasty! Give us a bite of that there pasty! We be mortal hungry! We be a-dying down here!"*

Thomas looked down, and blow me! He
saw standing there, not knee high to him, a
little fellow dressed top to toe as a bal-man,
with a tiny hammer in his hand, and a tiny
borer tucked through his belt, and a tiny
candle in his hatcap, and he was looking at
Thomas's pasty with such ravenous longing
on his wrinkled old face that Thomas
couldn't help but feel sorry for him.

So Thomas held out the pasty for the little fellow to have the first bite, and snap! The little fellow in one bite took nearly all the pasty there was, except for the thick curve of crust with Thomas's dirty fingerprints on it. There was very little left on the crust for Thomas to nibble.

"Hey!" cried Thomas.

"I suppose you're wanting a wish," said the little fellow. "Fair enough. What will it be?"

Thomas thought how tired he was. "I wish it was time to go home!" he said.

"Sleep it out, then," said the little fellow.

The men finished eating and drinking,
and picked up their tools, and there was
Thomas fast asleep on the end of the bench.

"Let him be till we need him," said Jack
the tribute man. "He's new to the work."

So Thomas slept through half the
afternoon, and the rest of the day went
more quickly than the morning, and then he
could climb up the towering ladders and
gain the open air, and the good green grass.

"How was the pasty?" asked Birdy, as the troop of tinners came down to the ferry that evening.

"It was good, but there wasn't enough," said Thomas.

"I'll make you a man-sized one tomorrow," Birdy promised him.

Chapter Three

So the next day Thomas had a pasty as big as any man jack of them, and he put it in his bag, and trudged up the hill to the mine.

The work was as hard as ever, and he was just as hungry and miserable when at last it was croust time, and he sat on the end of the bench and unwrapped his pasty.

He was just about to take a bite, when he heard again, *"Not so fast! Not so hasty! give us a bite of that there pasty! We be mortal hungry! We be a-dying down here!"* and blow me! There at his side, and no higher than the top of his knees, were two little fellows, all kitted out as miners, and looking so pined and hungry he couldn't help but feel sorry for them.

So he held out the pasty to them, but he said, "Just one bite each, mind. There has to be something for me!"

And snip, snap, right away the two little fellows took two tremendous bites, and the pasty was gone right down to the dry hard crust!

"Hey!" cried Thomas.

"He'll be wanting a wish, now," said the little fellows to each other. "What'll it be, Thomas?"

Thomas thought how he hated the dark. "I'm feared of the blackness down here," he said. "I wish I could see the daylight."

"Come come come," they said, and tugging at his shirt and trousers they dragged him away from the others, through a mazy twisty path of passageways, till they got him to a place where there was a pale disc of light on the floor, and a dusty beam standing up from it.

"Lookey up, lookey up!" they cried, and Thomas looked up, and he saw very far above him, at the top of a towering shaft, a round blue platter made of sky. It wasn't what he wanted at all, but he'd had his wish in a way, so that was that.

"How was the pasty?" Birdy asked him as he trudged home past her door that evening.

"It was good, but there wasn't enough," he told her. He was fair gnawing his knuckles for hunger.

"I'll make you a bigger one tomorrow," Birdy promised him.

Chapter Four

Well, the next day Thomas's pasty was
twice as long and twice as wide as anyone
else's, and as thick as a feather pillow. He
couldn't get it into his croust-bag, and
Birdy had to wrap it in a flour sack and
sling it over his back for him. It felt good
and warm, and heavy against his back, and
the savour of it from the neck of the sack
dangling by his shoulder was mainly good!

The tinners all laughed when they saw it.
"Who are you feeding, besides us?" they
asked. "You be fair greedy for such a
runtle!"

But Thomas thought it best not to tell them, and they didn't keep teasing him long. So at croust time, when the little voice as his knee piped up, saying *"Not so fast! Not so hasty! Give us a bite of that there pasty! We be mortal hungry! We be a-dying down here!"*, Thomas cheerfully took up his great big pasty in his two hands, and held it out to the little fellow.

And blow me! All at once there was half a dozen of them, all jumping up and taking a bite, and the pasty was gone right down to the crust again, before Thomas could shout "Hey!"

"What about me?" he said, crossly.

"You get a wish," said one of the little men.

Thomas thought how hungry he felt. "I'd wish for a nice fat pasty," he said.

"Lookey see," said the first little fellow. "There's what Buccas can do and what they can't do. What they can't do is fashion food. Try again."

"I wish I worked by the sea," said Thomas, for he was thinking how the fishermen didn't have to share their pilchard pies with greedy great talking mackerel.

"Come, come, come!" cried the little fellows all at once, and they pulled and tugged at Thomas's shirt and trousers, and then fair lifted him off his feet, and rushed him away with them, feet first, round and about and always downwards, through tiny tunnels where the roof scraped the skin off his nose as they went.

Down and down they carried him, till they reached the lowest level – the adit, where the waters of the earth drained out of the mine in a dark rushing stream, stained red by the tin ore washing down in it.

The Buccas didn't stop for a minute, but waded into the rushing water, and carried Thomas along until they were at the outfall, where the adit broke out of the cliff face, and spilled all the waters into the sea.

On the very brink they put him down, with his head spinning, and there he stood, with the cliff towering above him, and plunging below him, and the sea spread out below. A gull came winging by him, and he could see a boat far out.

So Thomas had his wish, but it wasn't what he wanted at all. It was a desperately dangerous place to be standing, even if your head wasn't spinning and your heart hammering. Thomas barely looked at the sea, but went down on his knees in the water, and scrambled back up the adit, getting soaking wet as he went, and a long way it did seem! And then when he reached dry ground he had to yammer and cry, before someone came to find him, for he was very lost.

"How did you get down there for blessed sake?" Jack the tribute man asked him.

But Thomas didn't like to say. "I missed my way," he said.

Going home that evening, Thomas was so faint with hunger he could hardly walk.

Standback Jack had a word with him on the way. "It doesn't do, you'll find," he said to Thomas kindly, "to eat a hefty morsel at croust time. It weighs you down. No wonder you feel queasy. Have a modest bite, and keep your hunger for your supper time. That way you'll be nimble all day. Trust me for it."

Thomas could have wept with the
unfairness of it! And here was Birdy,
coming up the path to meet him, to find
how he had got on. She could see at once
there was something wrong.

"What's amiss, Thomas?" she asked him.

"I'm *hungry!*" he wailed at her. Well, by
good luck she had a bannock in her apron
pocket, made up with the scraps of the
dough, that her mother had given her for
her tea. Thomas wolfed it in one bite, and
felt better.

"How was the pasty?" asked Birdy.

"I don't know!" cried Thomas. "There wasn't enough!"

"There's something the matter with you, Thomas!" said Birdy. "We've fed mortal many bal-men and bal-maidens twice your size and more, and they've always been staunched and pleased with the fare!"

So Thomas told her about the Buccas.

"And there wasn't any carrot left in your part?" Birdy asked him. "And there wasn't any onion? And there wasn't a morsel of tatties, or a taste of the gravy?"

"Nothing left but the crust," he told her, miserably. "And most of that had my fingerprints on it, and couldn't be eaten."

"Couldn't you tell them no?" Birdy asked him.

"You should see them, Birdy. They looked so ravened and wretched and starvling, you couldn't deny them a bite, when you've your hands full of food."

"We've got to think of something, Thomas," Birdy said, "or you'll starve to death. I'll ask my mother and father."

"We must bake him a famously larger pasty, then," said Birdy's mother.

"Doesn't do to get across a fairy miner," said Birdy's father. "And they could do with some Buccas' luck up there. The tin lode is nearly worked out, and there won't be livings for much longer."

Chapter Five

Well, the next morning, when the tinners came by, there was a wheel-barrow waiting for Thomas. And atop of the barrow was a pasty that was six foot across, and as thick as a mattress! It had taken the oven for itself, and filled the space that cooked six-dozen loaves on a normal morning. It was wrapped in a sack with a rope and pulley tied round it, ready to lower down the shaft, for it was larger by far than a lad could hope to carry.

"You be horrible greedy, Prentice Jack!" said Hefty Jack to Thomas. "You can't eat that by yourself, and that's a fact. Nobody could."

"Even the giant Tregeagle couldn't eat that much at a sitting!" said FireJack. "You should be ashamed to try on such a guzzle!"

But there wasn't much spark in their teasing – it was a bad sort of a morning.

At the top of the shaft, Jack the tribute man lined up his men, and he told them, "We've worked all the tin in our tunnels, boys, and if we don't find a new and likely lode very shortly we'll all be gone overseas before Christmas. Keep your eyes skinned for a gleam or a glint, every one of you."

Thomas was busy lowering his pasty down the shaft till he reached the place where they were working. He left it beside the water barrel, and the croust-bags of the others, and went to work. He really thought there might be a bite for him, this time.

But when the work was half done, and
they tramped back to their benches for their
croust time, a strange sight met Thomas's
eyes. There was his great pasty, propped up
on four chunks of granite, and there sitting
cross-legged round it, as though it had been
a table, were a dozen or more of the
Buccas, their napkins tucked under their
chins, and their knives and forks at the
ready.

"Yum yum yum, let's all have some!"
they cried, and as Thomas reached out to
break a piece for himself they all began to
eat, and the pasty was gone in a trice,
leaving just a seated ring of the little fellows
and heap of crust crumbs.

"Thieves! *Thieves!*" cried Thomas in a
rage. "That's my pasty you've taken! And
I'm HUNGRY!"

"You never are!" said FireJack, who was
sitting next to Thomas on the bench. "Have
you gobbled up all that vasty pasty? You'll
be ill!"

Thomas put his head in his hands. It was clear to him that none of his mates could see or hear the Buccas, that they were a torment just for him alone.

There were his team, all sitting around him. Their clothes were damp and dusty, and their faces sticky with sweat. And they were quiet and dejected today, as each man thought about leaving Cornwall behind, and going to far away lands where there might be more tin to be found, and a miner could cut a living for himself out of the hard rock.

Thomas felt a little tug on his sleeve.
"Have a wish, Thomas," said the first little
fellow. "We owe you a wish, and we
always pay our debts."

Thomas thought how mournful his mates
were feeling. "I'd like tin," he said. "Find us
a likely lode — we need tin."

And to his amazement there was the little
fellow shouting "Huzzah!" and dancing
around like a spinning top or a boy on a
birthday.

"We thought you'd never ask!" he said, "Come come, look and see ..." and he began tugging Thomas along by handfuls of his clothes, and his friends all pushing and pulling with him.

It was only a little way they dragged and carried Thomas, and then they set him down in the darkness, where only the candle in his cap shed a glimmer, and put his hammer in his hands, and said, "Try there!"

Thomas swung the hammer, and struck
where the little fellow pointed, and a great
tumble-down of rock fell out of the wall,
and showed him behind it a tunnel, all
made and ready, and in the walls of the
tunnel as far as his candle-light fell the lode
of tin was running, ready to cut. The little
fellows didn't use gunpowder, he could see,
but the bore holes were all made and ready.

"All for you, Thomas, all for you!" the Buccas were crying, and cavorting round his feet, and up and down their lovely likely lode. And as they danced they were flickering in his eyes, and turning sea-blue, and transparent as fire, until all he could see was a ring of dancing blue flames, guttering and blowing out as they moved away from him into the dark.

Thomas rubbed his eyes and went to fetch the others.

Chapter Six

There was a fair mountain of ingots made from the tin in that tunnel. Prentice Jack, that's to say, Thomas, had a due share, and a fine share it was. He and his mates stayed in Cornwall, and stayed lucky for many a year. They changed Thomas's name to Prospect Jack, because he was so good at finding tin.

And soon he didn't need to go hacking and heaving and carrying down the mine, but built himself a fine house in St Ives, and lived at ease.

But once a month, or thereabouts, he would get up early in the morning, and off he would go to the ferry. Birdy and her mother would have ready an oven-busting pasty, balanced on a barrow, and Thomas would pay for it with a golden guinea.

Then he would trundle it up the hillside, and lower it away down the mine-shaft. If anyone asked him about it his answer was pat and ready.

"I'm a man that pays my debts," he would say. "And there's some that can't fashion food, but that *loves* to get their teeth into a good Cornish pasty!"

Another title by award-winning author Jill Paton Walsh from Wayland …

Birdy and the Ghosties
Illustrated by Alan Marks

She looked once, and she saw the terrible ghosties …

Sometimes Birdy watches her father row people across the dangerous sea, but when the wrinkled old woman asks to be ferried across, Birdy jumps in too. The woman tells Birdy she has second sight, but Birdy isn't sure she wants this special gift. However, soon she finds that looking twice at things can bring the most unexpected results …

Lively and engaging, with short chapters and illustrations throughout in colour and black-and-white, this is another wonderful story set in Cornwall, ideal for newly confident readers.

"A master storyteller whose characters spring off the page and into life." *Oxford Times*

WAYLAND

These Gripping Tales are short, accessible novels for newly confident readers.

Gripping Tales

Fair's *Fair*

LEON GARFIELD

Gripping Tales

The **Thief's Daughter**

ALAN MARKS

Gripping Tales

Emily's *Legs*

DICK KING-SMITH

Gripping Tales

Thomas *and the* **Tinners**

JILL PATON WALSH

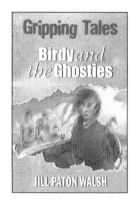

Gripping Tales

Birdy *and the* **Ghosties**

JILL PATON WALSH

Gripping Tales

The **King** *in the* **Forest**

MICHAEL MORPURGO

Gripping Tales

The **Shoemaker's Boy**

JOAN AIKEN